I0591099

Praise for From *Bitter to Better: A Chocolate Momma's Journey to Self-Discovery*

Bold and decadent..this novella, authored by Karen Taylor Bass, is a must-read for women of all ages. A guilty pleasure, you will continue to savor the flavor of each chapter as you digest the heartfelt relationship nuggets offered by Bass and the women who are charter members of the Chocolate Mama's Club (CMC).

- **Cynthia M. Horner**
  CEO, RIGHT ON! Digital
  Editor-In-Chief, *RIGHT ON!* Magazine
  CEO, Cinnamon Chips Media

Praise for From *Bitter to Better: A Chocolate Momma's Journey to Self-Discovery*

This book takes you on a journey from the passenger seat of heartache, trauma, resilience, tenacity, and triumph-all while being inside the head of the main character while she reflects and navigates the difficult stages of each step she must take. I love how the book integrates her close friendships, stressing the importance of having a tribe...I can't wait for the next book! (I hope this will be a series!)
- Michelle M.

Praise for From *Bitter to Better: A Chocolate Momma's Journey to Self-Discovery*

Karen Taylor Bass bravely shares her highest ties and lowest lows with her readers. Her story resonates with women from all walks of life. She makes the reader contemplate their own journey. Karen reminds us all that life has ups and downs. Those downs are made easier by the people who truly care for us. Sisterhood is sweeter than chocolate!
- S. Wilkins

Praise for From *Bitter to Better: A Chocolate Momma's Journey to Self-Discovery*

This book journey is a cathartic experience when you see yourself or someone you know reflected in its pages and characters. Perfect for those experiencing a midlife renaissance, it highlights the lack of a playbook and the essential role of sisterhood and friendship! It offers insightful parallels for navigating life from various female perspectives. Engaging and effortless to read, I couldn't put this down. I can't wait for the series!

- LBD

Praise for From *Bitter to Better: A Chocolate Momma's Journey to Self-Discovery*

I really couldn't put this book down. Karen Taylor Bass has created characters that are so relatable. You become invested quickly in the lives of these Chocolate Mommas. So much that you can't wait to find out how things turn out for these women. Definitely 10/10!
- **Pascale**

This book was wonderfully written. I started reading it and could not put it down. Great Novella for a Saturday afternoon!!!!
- **Janet. M. Taylor**

Loved this book. The author's note really reveals how this book is for all women! Journey through your life and friends with these characters. So relatable!
- **Agnes D.**

Praise for From *Bitter to Better*: A Chocolate Momma's Journey to Self-Discovery

"From Bitter to Better" is the kind of story that you can't put down. Each page is a rollercoaster of emotions, drawing you in and making you feel every bit of the journey. Karen's writing is so vivid and engaging that I could see the scenes playing out like a movie in my mind. Hollywood, are you listening? This needs to be on the big screen! The CMC is here for it! The novella's characters are richly developed and oh-so-real. They remind us that we are not alone in our struggles and that there's always a path from bitter to better – Chocolate Pages! So good you want to eat them!

- Dr. Pam Perry

From Bitter To Better

A Chocolate Momma's Journey to Self-Discovery

(Volume I)

Also by Karen Taylor Bass

You Want Caviar but Have Money For Chitlins:
A Smart Do-It-Yourself PR Guide for Those on a Budget

30 Day Reset: Brand, Business & Bottom-Line

The Brand New Mommy: From Babies To Branding To Bliss
(Learn How To Renew your Life)

US: $24.95
CANADA: $29.16

Copyright © 2025 Taylor Made Media Books

All rights reserved. No part of this publication may be reproduced, distributed, or transmitted in any form or by any means, including photocopying, recording, or other electronic or mechanical methods, without the prior written permission of the publisher, except in the case of brief quotations embodied in critical reviews and certain other noncommercial uses permitted by copyright law. For permission requests, write to the publisher, addressed "Attention: Permissions Coordinator," at the address below.

ISBN: 978-0-9759106-6-5 (Paperback)

Library of Congress Control Number: 2025910612

Any references to historical events, real people, or real places are used fictitiously. Names, characters, and places are products of the author's imagination.

Front cover illustration generated by Adobe Firely.
Yoga illustrations by AndrewBassDesign.
Book design by AndrewBassDesign.

Published by

BOOKS

TaylorMade Media Books
Distributed by Ingram Sparks
City of Publication - La Vergne, Tennessee
2nd Edition, June 2025

Karen Taylor Bass
karen@karentaylorbass.com

www.karentaylorbass.com

a novella

From Bitter To Better

A Chocolate Momma's Journey to Self-Discovery

(Volume I)

Karen Taylor Bass

Dedication:

This book is for my beautiful young people, Sebastian and Sofia, family, friends, clients, and everyone who hugged me when I needed it most. My heart is good because this book allowed me to release and give myself grace. Most importantly, this book is dedicated to my ancestors, especially my grandmother, great aunt, uncle, and all my guardian angels. Thank you, God, for blessing me with a badass Jamaican mom who challenged me to become fearless. And, a special shout out to the sweetest angels who held me up when I was tired and afraid.

For Aunt Shirley, Juanita Stephens, and Angelo Ellerbee.

Rest in Paradise Juanita Stephens and Eileen 'Aunt Peaches' Brown.

Author's Note:

From *Bitter To Better: A Chocolate Momma's Journey to Self-Discovery* is raw and contains the emotions and experiences of my four-year journey. The words on the book's pages were written in real-time to capture the authenticity of this grown woman's journey. I ask for your grace when reading, and know that life is not perfect. However, it is much sweeter with chocolate, and when you tell it like it is.

"De nigger woman is de mule uh de world so fur as Ah can see."

– Zora Neale Hurston, *Their Eyes Were Watching God*

Prologue

It is not something we talk about, but it keeps us hostage. Trauma takes up an incredible amount of space in our brain and body. It only needs a simple opening, and like the wild dandelion, it takes root and flourishes like a weed. We all have trauma, some worse than others. Most of it is generational. No experience is necessary: it comes with you at birth. Your mom, dad, grandparents, and so forth carried it and passed it down to you. Think of trauma as the inheritance you don't want.

Trauma was my old story. I arrived when my mom was eighteen. My grandparents and Aunt Peaches raised me for the first five years of my life. My daddy was an older man, established in his career, but also an alcoholic. His mom died in childbirth, and his dad died years later. He was broken and presumably gutted. I inherited my parent's stuff the moment I was conceived, and that is the gift of trauma. For me, add the anxiety of leaving Jamaica and coming to America, postpartum depression at 40, divorce, and starting over again in life at age 55.

On the other hand, I have (also) experienced so much good shit in life: my career; family; friends; marriage; a bonus son; the birth of my daughter at 40; and Yoga. The really good stuff encouraged me to fight through and reinvent, reset, pivot, and surrender. Your mind creates whatever you need for each chapter of your life. I started Chocolate Mommas in 2019, the same year I became a certified Yoga instructor. I broke the generational trauma in my lineage, which is not an easy dragon to slay. Shit, it almost took me down, but God kept me the entire time.

With grace,
Your Chocolate Momma

The Birth of a Chocolate Momma

A fresh start was on the menu. Although I had talked about it, and even fantasized about the notion of divorcing, selling my home, and starting over, it seemed just a dream. When it actually happened, I had no idea what to do. In all honesty, fear halted my movements, a metaphor for much of my life, which I care not to admit. FEAR - False Emotions Appearing Real, courtesy of Iyanla Vanzant (the guru in my head). In many ways, fear has paralyzed me to live my best life. I remember when I wanted to relocate to Los Angeles, and my grandmother convinced me otherwise. Reflecting on it, as much as I loved my grandmother, although she was protective of me, she also kept me in *fear*. I know she meant well, but when your exposure and your experience is limited, you tend to follow the path which keeps everything status quo. This is why I always reserve judgment about others; one only works with what they know, which is okay.

The lessons I learned over the years from ancestral love, mentors, elders, friends, and traveling brought me to this place right now: a new beginning; a new state; a new home; and a new journey. I choose to stay open and optimistic about the future. Regardless, I know for sure a space for mommas to come together is more necessary than ever. If you don't have any Chocolate Mommas, heed these words: you will *always* need chocolate and mommas during the great, not-so-great, and the fucked-up times.

Meet my Chocolate Mommas, affectionately called CMs.

The Chocolate Momma

T his book is dedicated to women in their 40's and 50's. The mavericks and renaissance women; the shy girl finding her voice and power; and the sister holding on yet unsure which direction to turn. When the mystical 4-0 arrives, life changes. You reflect on everything you heard, learned, and believed. For many, the magic touch is waning. Self-doubt has crept in because you are not where you want to be. Some shit has happened repeatedly, causing you to question *everything*. Others are badasses and rock stars, respectively. The bottom line is this: as you age, you no longer want to hide from yourself. You are ready to unpack childhood trauma, losses, bad relationships, not-so-good jobs, re-evaluate friendships, lovers, and all the causes of former suffering. This is what happened to me once I turned 50. To deal with it all, I created a tribe to help me heal.

I love being a black woman, a chocolate woman, and a proud Caribbean Jamaican sister who loves her African roots and is also a super proud mom of two. Only some people gain admission or receive an invitation into our sorority - the Chocolate Momma Club,

CMC - one for accomplished, down-to-earth, conscious, black and brown women.

The feeling of isolation, and desperation for some real face time with my sisters, caused me to start the CM. You see, I live in a world where I genuinely don't exist or matter, if you ask the establishment. My story is no different than Shannequa, Jane, Mia, Sofia, or Karen. My name happens to be Nia, and this is the crazy shit: every Black woman can relate to every word on this page. She is the person for whom I write. She is the person who I hold in my heart. She is the person who carries around her baggage and trauma each day, hoping for a safe place to put it. She is me, and I finally dared to express and share it. This is my story and the tribe I created to heal and pivot.

If you are saying "Amen," then, shit, welcome to The Chocolate Momma Club. If you love chocolate, proud Black Queens, and are a stressed-out mom, you came to the right place.

Sadly, like all Queens, I forgot my unicorn status, and some time has passed since I put myself first and, indeed, exhaled. My soul - and sole - goal and purpose: to remind chocolate mommas they matter (even if society says otherwise), and the pledge is for sisters to uplift the other and shine a light on a fellow.

Daily, people ask, how do I join the sisterhood of CMC? Well, first you must be invited. Then, be a supportive, real sister-girl for admission into the club, filled with the most scintillating potluck and girl's night out. Oh yes, we love living, laughing, and telling our war stories because sharing is genuinely caring. Only a Black woman can understand the shit that makes this thing called life both fucking hard and sweet at the same time. This space is sacred. We have shared everything from divorce, bad credit, cancer, baby momma drama, and crazy-ass hubbies. Daily challenges are real, and only God and your chocolate momma sister can help you overcome anything. Yes, *anything*!

There are few words in the lexicon which excite me more than love, confidence, sex, power, and gratitude. Words like chocolate (I have a sweet tooth) and momma (beautiful on the inside and out) always give me a reason to pause and celebrate – *no matter what.*

CMC Creed: "Chocolate Mommas living, loving, supporting, and nurturing their whole selves. We want Agape love, joy, and bliss! Life is challenging, but daily, I promise to live, love, laugh, smile and be a good person. We are sisters, affectionately called Chocolate Mommas!

Meet the members of CMC:

Nia Morris (glue, nucleus, in a fucked-up marriage, mom of two)

Winnie Scott (militant, married to younger man, mom of four)

Whitley DuBois (pedigree, pill popper, anxiety-ridden, always on a diet, skinny, adopted)

Jessica Reese (white girl, hippie, happily married, mom of three)

Christie BonTemp (firefighter, great spirit, two years to retirement, happily married, mother of two)

Zora Love (baby momma, recently met the man of her dreams, mother of one)

Linda Chong (Trump supporter, funny, no children and divorced)

Nia Morris

Nia is the absolute bomb and the nucleus of the group: 50; sun-kissed bronze skin; personality to light up any room, confidence; teeth like chiclets; natural mane like Diana Ross (but hers is real); stylish; *and* a successful businesswoman. A proud Jamaican-born woman, who can annunciate the s-h-iii-t out of any word and assures everyone knows it, she is also a fantastic mother. Another thing: Nia and her hubby have not had sex in over five years. How does she cope?

Wine, tequila, her Chocolate Mommas, work, vacations, spa retreats, vibrator, and her fingers - which qualifies as reason enough to walk out of the marriage. There is so much to Nia, but she is learning about herself. She does not yet recognize how strong, smart, powerful, and resilient she is and will become. Nia is like many women, not understanding their gift or power because they have been too busy handling or solving everyone else's problems. Her self-discovery somehow started with a reintroduction to Yoga and the dissolution of her marriage.

Winnie Scott

Winnie is the wife to the handsome, young, and charismatic Chief of Detectives in Elmont and Winnie is no slouch either at 52. She is a beauty: tall; chocolate with blond dreadlocks; dimples, diamond-like teeth with a smile to open the heavens; and a personality as fancy-free as a four-year-old. The Chocolate Mommas love Winnie. She is our feel-good sister. If you are ever down, saddled with doubt and fear, the first person to call is Winnie. She will remix and transform your spirit with her magical fairy dust. I must caution you however - just because you smile and can turn a frown upside down, doesn't mean you avoid issues and problems. Winnie has had her share of childhood drama and PTSD, not to mention narrowly escaping a fucked-up relationship with her first husband.

She vowed never to settle for pain or sorrow again because that shit was simply *non-negotiable*. Winnie left her crazy ass husband with a baby in hand from Somewhere USA and settled in Elmont with a mission and purpose to never look back. The Chocolate Mommas never asked Winnie about her past life. They just knew it was their business only to know what to know. Real friendship is knowing every-body got shit they are working through, and sisters have earned the right to create, manipulate, and tell their truth how they see fit. What we do know from Winnie is this: once upon a time, she served in the United States Navy and retired after twenty years. She meticulously created a new life - one that makes her feel safe, happy, and loved, which is good enough for us. I know you might think this makes no sense, but who are we to judge? The reason we created this group was to be naked, honest, and who/what we always wanted to be:

Free. Black. Beautiful. Chocolate. Mommas.

How It All Started

Nia was losing all her marbles one moment at a time. She had just dropped off her son at junior high school, navigated the traffic to drop off her toddler at nursery school, hoping she could make it on time so she could cry and crumble in peace. No such luck this morning. The traffic Gods had already decided there was no place for crying and falling apart today; it would have to wait for another day. Nia reached the exclusive nursery school, *The First Milestone*, at 8:30 am. She was still dealing with postpartum depression, and getting out of bed every day was a task, but today, she was determined to have one last cry, just one more. It was time to get to rebuilding and start living. Today felt different though. She couldn't put her finger on it, but Nia knew something floated in the air. The day felt fresh like a cleansing gust of wind; a new beginning; a different lens; or a sign from above. She half smiled, thinking, "Maybe I can find other moms searching, like me and create a support system - with cocktails."

For the first time in a long time, Nia looked at her toddler, hugged her tightly, and reassured her baby they would be alright - better than alright, they would overcome this and everything else. After fifteen months, Nia finally had the energy to sprint up the steps with her daughter and hand her over to Miss LaVerne at *The First Milestone*. Just at that moment, as she was leaving, Nia saw another mom, one who looked familiar. She was stylish and the perfect shade of cocoa, bright-eyed, with a flawless smile, and jet black hair outlined like a halo. They had never spoken before, but today, her sadness was like Nia's. The moms' eyes connected as they left their toddlers in good hands. At that moment, Whitley DuBois introduced herself to Nia.

Today was the beginning of something: The Chocolate Momma Club.

Whitley DuBois

The day they met on the steps at *The First Milestone*, Nia and Whitley forged a genuine sister-girl connection, but all that glitters is not gold. Whitley, like Nia, found herself navigating postpartum depression - seemingly living a life of perfection, but actually barely hanging on with crazy glue. Whitley was genuinely breathtaking; she was beyond beautiful. Although petite and wore a weave, her body was toned, lean - in close competition with Angela Bassett. She was fly: as the kids say, "Facts." Whitley was aware of her beauty, but that hair was kind of, well, crunchy. Like most women with access and money, Whitley believed she had to have a long weave with blond highlights to validate her place in society. Her natural 'fro only made a cameo appearance during morning drop-off at *The First Milestone*.

Who doesn't want to have some of that Beyonce Beehive mystique? Whitley was a reality TV junkie and followed the philosophy that everything light and blonde was right. I can't blame her, though. She was adopted by a white family at the age of seventeen months. Her parents did their absolute best, but she experienced no real interaction with black folk, until she arrived at Emory University in Atlanta, which made her feel somewhat out of place as it relates to the black diaspora. Whitley was certainly pedigree. Her mother was a trust fund baby, and her father was a world-renowned anthropologist and university professor. Whitley didn't hunger for material things, just something harder to come by: acceptance and love. I guess it's why we bonded. Many of us walk around in pain, and pain recognizes pain.

Although I don't come from money, I, too, yearn for acceptance from my biological mother. The only difference is that I am not out here poppin pills or starving myself to escape the pain like Whitley. The crazy thing about life is that we repeat the trauma and pattern of what we know. Whitley was obsessed with climbing the corporate ladder. Everything she acquired was simply an accessory, just like her adopted daughter, Brittney. Somewhere deep down, Whitley was just like me, a woman searching for acceptance. Maybe, just maybe, I could create a safe space for us to heal. Like Whitley, I was thankful for that chance encounter on the steps.

Don't Give Up

Nia expressed a longstanding desire for a baby, specifically a girl. Carrying this wish and prayer in her heart, the day she missed her period brought the doubt it might be happening. Nia reflected on an abortion a decade ago, pondering if she had missed her opportunity. Before the arrival of her precious Taylor, Nia conceived a baby in her late 20s with an ex. She describes him as a bald, chocolate man, intelligent on paper, charismatic, a ladies' man, and a skillful lover. Despite his shortcomings, Nia acknowledged the intimacy of their relationship was always yummy.

Nia admitted the relationship with this man never honestly had a chance, built as it was on a foundation of good sex and even better sex. She reflected on the impact of trauma and the cyclical nature of its influence until one chooses to take a different path. Despite reservations, the man became Nia's fiancé, a path she realized they should never have taken. Acknowledging the challenges of bad decisions and love-seeking, Nia shared the discovery of her pregnancy with him and rebuffed the initial suggestion that they keep the baby.

After accepting the finality of the relationship, Nia chose to terminate the pregnancy. She asserted that this decision was hers to make and hers only. The first pregnancy resulted in a boy. However, two decades later, when Nia became pregnant with her then-husband, she learned the sex of the baby: a girl. Nervous and hopeful the previous abortion would not affect a safe delivery, complications arose due to a weakened cervix coupled with the problem of placenta previa, placing Nia under a doctor's order for bed rest until the scheduled C-section for delivery. The delivery of Taylor with all the complications and the two blood transfusions almost took everything from Nia. She fought to become a mother, to stay alive, to raise her baby girl, and to save her marriage, and then one day, she stopped fighting and started to become bitter.

Just Anxious

Anxious, much? Nia traversed a life overshadowed by anxiety, a constant companion cleverly disguised as mere nerves. Whether delivering speeches, conversing with adults, or facing a classroom, the persistent unease manifested in sweaty palms, a racing heart, and a somersaulting stomach. Unaware her experience was more than typical nerves, she assumed everyone faced what she felt.

As society gradually embraced mental health transparency, Nia engaged in a perpetual negotiation with her brain, attempting to maintain calmness and hold triggers at bay. The birth of her daughter at age 40 marked a pivotal moment, introducing a new word into her lexicon – "anxious." According to Merriam-Webster's Dictionary, anxious was defined as "extreme uneasiness of mind or brooding fear: worried." To Nia, it mostly translated into feeling powerless.

A high-risk pregnancy due to her age added another layer of stress. Balancing work as a consultant for a non-profit arts center, managing her own business, navigating office politics, and negotiating strained marital ties heightened Nia's anxiety. Her pregnancy coasted smoothly until a disastrous babymoon in the Dominican Republic: marred by discomfort, disruption in the womb, tasteless food, and scorching sun. Upon returning home, Nia's fears materialized as she began to bleed, prompting an urgent visit to the hospital. The diagnosis; Placenta Previa, a nightmare for any expecting mother. Admitted to the hospital, her appearance and concerns became additional stressors, compounded by the unpredictability which often accompanies those with melanin in their skin.

The subsequent week in the hospital, filled with tests, prodding, and a compromised brand image, yielded a battleground against panic. Prayer warriors, including her grandmother, great aunt, and God, served as her allies. Despite the doctor's gloomy predictions, Nia asserted her confidence, rejecting the notion that her premature baby would end up in the neonatal unit.

The scheduled C-section brought a mix of excitement and nervousness, or, as the young people say, "nerve-cited." Despite a successful delivery and a daughter thriving, Nia awakened feeling weak, sensing something was amiss. A nurse's concern about hemorrhaging due to Placenta Previa escalated into a life-threatening situation, with Nia continuing to advocate for herself in critical moments.

Surviving the night with the help of blood transfusions, Nia finally met her baby girl, crying tears of gratitude. Her post-delivery self, however, was marked by more anxiety and insecurity. Despite being thankful for the skilled medical professionals who saved her life, she grappled with doubt. She posed an unusual question about blood transfusions, hinting at an internal struggle in her mind, body, and soul.

Husbands Ain't Shit

The Chocolate Mommas had some hubbies who weren't "all that *or worth a bag* of chips." Somewhere between "I Do," banging sex, and date night, misery appeared. Was it the notion of introducing children, losing your job, or staying at home to raise the kids? I mean, the word sacrifice is often used in marriage.

However, it manifests itself as a liability down the line. The married Chocolate Mommas in the group are often unhappy. Their husbands suck. If there were a blame game, they would win the grand prize. CMC hubbies are jealous of their wives. Somehow, they have tried mightily to suck the life, pride, joy, and bliss out of their partners and, essentially, keep them in a state of flux and insecurity. If one husband, just one, publicly supported his wife, showered some love or stopped fucking around with a neighbor, maybe less depression, anxiety, and medication would be needed for these sisters.

I remember the day my man and I exchanged vows - what a glorious day. I wanted to be married; I wanted to have a child; I wanted a big chunk of that American dream. The truth is, many women who marry later in life are often more set in their character and beliefs, and their ways. Marriage actually occurs to appease the family and to legitimize any children. This describes me: my insides fluttered like butterflies, but, against my better judgment, I said, "I do."

I learned quickly that for men, the phrase "for better or worse," meant "As long as I can live my lifestyle, it can work." Not to throw my hubby under the bus, but when we married, I was the breadwinner in the driver's seat. When it ended, he carried me for years until he felt burdened. Yes. Husbands, indeed, ain't shit. Somehow, they have a time limit on how long they can support you, without facing any setbacks. I've concluded that men don't want the *entire* woman, just the good, dependable shit. When the warranty is up, you better still own some good parts.

Each member of the CMC has a similar story: a momma once on top of her game until the birth of her child; then left reeling to the core afterwards. It started with depression, isolation, and the blaming game, and then, one day, you realized this *could not* continue and an intervention was needed.

The moment we realized our war stories were similar, was the day each member of CMC truly gave herself a chance to heal, exhale, breathe, and live - without permission. The moment you rediscover your essence, magic, breath, smile, and laughter is when you start to accept your authentic self. Each member of our club is healing one day at a time. We are not the same mom that walked into that first potluck cocky, curt, and over-compensating. The truth is, when you start to uncover the pain, you realize that having a shitty husband ain't nothing. You can't blame someone else for your shit. Healing is owning *all* your stuff.

Nobody Cares

"The truth of the matter," Nia said to the members of CMC, "Is that nobody cares." All eight members looked at one another and reaffirmed the statement of their fierce leader with a neck roll, eye roll, and finger snap. Whitney said, "I guess I keep hoping someone in my household will realize that I am sad and depressed and ask me how I'm doing?" Nia, however, could not take the pity party any longer; she exchanged an exasperated look with Zora, Christie, Linda, and Jessica, the other members of CM. Nia looked at her watch and said, "Ladies, it is 9 pm, and we are supposed to be exhaling. Instead, we are sitting here talking about the same mutha-fuckas that don't care two shits about us. I say we get out of here, go to Freeport, listen to some Jazz, have a round of drinks and appetizers, and just accept that it's our fault. We stopped caring about us."

At that moment, the ladies were quiet, numb. They had spent so much time, hours, seconds, minutes, days, and years - waiting for validation - they forgot to matter *to themselves*. They had become Betty Freakin' Crocker, and Aunt Jemima all rolled into one. From the spotless home to the manicured lawn to the daily, delicious custom pancakes they made for their kids, and the well-thought-out lunches with just the correct ratio of protein to carbs and saturated fat, they sacrificed themselves daily. Let's not forget the color-coordinated napkins and delicious, delectable dinner recipes from the master Chef JJ Johnson, right out of the pages of *Between Harlem and Heaven* cookbook. Sadly, perfection does not matter and is truly overrated. All these Chocolate Mommas were, once upon a time, the dopest bitches in Corporate America - they owned the game.

You heard right; every Chocolate Momma had permeated the glass ceiling – handling mega budgets and staff and making bottom-line decisions, all while managing to stay flawless, sexy, current, and open to endless opportunities. It seemed like a lifetime ago, like once upon a time. Nia, Winnie, Whitley, Jessica, Zora, Christie, and Linda had become a shell of their former selves. They had forgotten to put on their oxygen mask and put themselves first. Men love the women with whom they exchange vows and marry. The uber-strong, confident person from their wedding day, not the indecisive, insecure woman who has forgotten self and power as time elapses. Secretly, husbands want us to be selfish; they want us to have a life, and the minute we give up everything for the family, we no longer become sexy, desirable, and wanted. Yeah, nobody cares when you sacrifice, except for your Chocolate Mommas.

Every Group Has One

Nia didn't care much for Jessica Reese. Jessica was the obligatory white girl in the group and only because Nia felt generous the day Christie asked if her friend could also join. It was just like Christie, always needing a security blanket (more on that later), and - bam! - Jessica entered our circle. Jessica could bake her ass off, though. She was happily married with three children, a little sneaky, average height, cute, blonde sporting shoulder-length hair like Drew Barrymore, and a true hippie until anyone questioned or threatened to compromise her rights. Yaaas. You know the type. She loved some black people and Chocolate Mommas, but you had to be careful around her because she was always keenly watching what you owned, what your children wore, and why she didn't have what you had.

On the flip side, Jessica's hubby, Leo, was the *coolest*. He had swag for a white boy, was smooth, charismatic, and consistently expressed unique opinions when discussing race relations. The Chocolate Mommas enjoyed Leo; he eased the weight of Jessica's presence.

I didn't *dislike* Jessica; I grew up with her type both in school and corporate America. The white girl who loves and understands Black people, curious to get broken off by a strong brother, acts super cool and understanding but never truly rejoices for you if you receive a promotion or are lauded by the boss or teacher. She could be slippery, so we decided to keep her around, learn how to play her game and, eventually, the ultimate one - white America.

The Day Mommas Got Saved

There was something in the air on this crisp autumn day as the ladies prepared to meetup for brunch. The leaves were a rustic burnt orange, the ladies were walking to the train station with their heads held high on the outside, but something was coming through the body with each step. The heaviness of the shoulders could no longer be contained internally, the mommas were ready to release emotionally and today was the day. The Chocolate Mommas decided to leave Elmont, take the LIRR (Long Island Railroad) into Manhattan, and indulge in afternoon tea at The Pierre. This far exceeded just any afternoon tea; it was tea at the fancy Pierre Hotel, Sixty-first and Fifth Avenue, across from Central Park. Yaaaas! The Chocolate Mommas are dressed in their finest Sunday wear, drenched in, I *have more money and style than you. You better recognize that.*

You know the look: leather pants; jeans; fitted shirt; red bottoms; hair laid; makeup and jewelry popping. The girls came to shine today. It was time to let it all go: tea, scones, Bellini cocktails, and the finest french fries. Linda selected the venue, it was one of her favorites, and it was also her birthday. We decided to walk in individually to add some spice to the brunch because we all know how much energy and power Chocolate Mommas can bring - not to mention, everyone looked exquisite. Nia, Winnie, Whitley, Jessica, Christie, Zora, and Linda deserved to walk down that catwalk and step into the Tea Room at The Pierre, which is exactly what we did.

Once seated, we ordered, kee-kee'd, lifted our champagne flutes filled with a tasty peach Bellini, and toasted Linda on achieving a milestone birthday: 55 years and fabulous. Linda always looked like a million dollars, plus. She was worth more in actual currency and was a truly valuable friend. Linda exuded a royal air: the perfume was the finest limited edition from France; the wardrobe was tailored and unique to her size two body; the hair (all hers) dropped to her shoulders with a slight curl on the ends; and the body was toned, tight and muscular. Her previous incarnation as a swimmer shimmered off her lithe figure in waves. Linda's personality, sweet like maple syrup, enchanted us Chocolate Mommas. We rooted for her new love and exciting dating life. Her first marriage ended badly. Although she had no children, we all innately knew she had discovered the secret of youth – don't have children to drive you crazy or add years to your face and hairline. Real talk. Sssshiiit.

After toasting the birthday girl, something magical happened. Every Chocolate Momma broke down and took off her fake mask. The funny thing about real friendship is once the facade drops, we display who we really are - naked. Zora asked Nia what was happening with her marriage and how long before she put out the current wack-ass muthafucka? Seriously? She actually used those words? Everyone practically spit out or choked on their cocktails, while

Zora came hard for our leader. I mean, Nia was dope and all, but her marriage was fucked, and she needed to be called on the carpet by her fellow Chocolate Momma.

Nia was stunned. She sat quietly and reflectively, in a Nia kind of way. Her face looked somber; her words slow and difficult to express. She searched for them carefully; still confused and filled with disbelief. When she finally spoke she said, "I have the same thought every day. Every morning, I look at myself and feel like I stopped believing. My children look at me with disdain, they want to know how mommy could be so dope, but act so scared. I see their faces and I want to cry, each and every time. You know what really hurts? I am a strong woman, I fucking know better, and never believed I would be *here*. I am a black woman, leader, and change agent. And, this mutha-fucka has me sleeping downstairs in a twin bed, while he sleeps in our California King. How did I lose myself, cloak myself in fear and settle for basic shit?" I asked myself recently, "What was my motive? Was it my children, or am I just scared to be alone?" No one spoke a word; silence enveloped our table. What did our just leader say? Did she admit she was settling for the basics and uncomfortable ASF, while her husband slept in the big bed? *Hell nawh!* We got her back though, Chocolate Momma style. We looked at Nia with disbelief, recognizing this was happening in real-time. She said that life had been fucked up, and she made a wrong decision by staying with her husband; although the marriage ended seven years ago, she wanted to do better for her kids. Winnie and Whitley simultaneously screamed, "Gurlllll, you are too dope to be sleeping in a fucking twin bed. Tell that negro, shit is not going down like that, no mo'!"

Nia, Winnie, and Whitley started to cry, and one by one, Linda,

Zora, Jessica, and Christie began to bawl too. It started because of Nia, but now this was about *our* situation. Each Chocolate Momma carried a heavy burden, a personal burden, the burden of holding on to shit which no longer worked for or served us. Winnie shared what she faced. Whitley, Linda, Zora added their stories, each one of them contributing to the conversation, and so on until everyone spoke. Nia started the party with her revelation, but we all carried a cross to bear. Today was the day the Chocolate Mommas found salvation - in each other and in God. We came to Jesus, left all that shit at the altar, and laid down our burdens. Our sisters needed this afternoon's tea: dressed up and all, it was time to rip off the mask.

PTA Blues

Welcome to the elementary Parent Teachers Association (PTA), or what I love to call the Petty Tribe Assholes. The PTA had been Nia's second home with two children in the school, lending her volunteer skills for the past ten years. During her tenure there, Nia served as a general member and co-president. Eventually, she ran for School Board and won. She loved participating in a movement, making a difference, and giving her community a competitive edge. That is how the PTA felt in the beginning. A consortium of concerned moms and dads wanting to make a difference for their children, school, and community; lately, however, things shifted. The school welcomed new families left, right, and center, new principals, and the perennial members were either headed back to work, marriages in flux, or busily navigated their older children's high school or college life. Something different existed these days. Things changed and Nia wasn't having any of it. She ran for the Board to help the community, and her tolerance for petty bullshit equaled *zero*. Her tenure as a PTA executive board member was a thing of the past as she now wore a new hat as a Board of Ed member for the district. She looked at everything through a new lens and longed for the PTA of the past - a time when parents had space to care; they remembered to attend a monthly meeting. This particular gathering was yet another disappointing one, with no quorum again. Nia sat in the audience, keenly watching the body language, and realizing it was not the PTA of old - her mother's or hers.

Something was amiss. As a child, the PTA seemed like an organization of perfect moms with preparations and solutions for every question, issue, and celebration for the school, let alone the best-baked goods. Yes. These were the PTA memories Nia was clinging to and tried to restore with her crew of parents. She awoke from daydreaming and looked at the beautiful Chocolate Mommas in the room and on the executive board. They looked exhausted, barely hanging on to their sanity. Exhaustion was a familiar look for the PTA board, and Nia also knew about the "spent bug"- the feeling of erupting like a volcano, full of ideas but no workforce or volunteers to execute them, forget excellent baked goods. Nia did spot some boxed cookies and juice. She shook her head realizing these ladies in attendance needed a night out with the Chocolate Mommas, but Nia did not like the vibe from most of them, except one.

Christie Walker. Christie sat on the executive board, a retired firefighter, and genuinely seemed happy, not fake joyfulness. Her spirit was light, her children well-poised and polite, and when she talked about her husband, you wanted what she had. Nia knew that Christie would be a perfect fit for Chocolate Mommas. The club needed an energy remixer and catalyst. Someone happy to be with their husband and happy to be married. Adding Christie to CMC might motivate the Mommas, especially Nia, to gain the courage to practice self-care, self-love and remove negativity to usher in absolute peace, bliss, and happiness.

The Day She Came Alive

Nia knew deep in her heart she needed to make changes. Cue Sam Cooke's, *A Change Is Gonna Come*. Sixteen years in a loveless marriage, and with each year, she felt more and more less than her true self: less pretty; happy, less sharp. Her heart, however, felt brighter. A subtle change happened with Nia, and it started the night of her surprise birthday potluck. They caught their founder and leader off guard at Christie's house for a "PTA " meet-up, and she was utterly clueless when she arrived in black tights, an orange/white color block top, and booties. Nia had her folders, notebook, and pen - ready for a meeting. She looked different, though. Her hair had grown, which was new for her; thick and shoulder-length with burnt orange tips. This look favored her.

The crew started arriving individually with their culinary offerings: wine; champagne; and dirty stories. It was yummy and just what the doctor ordered, especially for the birthday girl. Nia laughed, smiled, and relaxed. Christie and Winnie brought out a scandalous birthday cake - a well-endowed Black dick saying, "Come Get It" with barely enough room for "Happy Birthday." It was amazing. Nia was surprised and started to cry. Shit, we all cried. We knew it was much more than champagne and scandalous cake which brought her to tears. In the spirit of true sisterhood, we encouraged her to release all of what she needed. We toasted, celebrated, and loved up on our girl, warrior, and leader. The food was delectable, the drinks even better, and we all felt nice after satisfying our stomachs and souls.

The stories are the best part of the night when Chocolate Mommas get together. The same night, a friend of Winnie mentioned a Black Yoga school had recently opened in Queens. Nia perked up and said she had always wanted to be a yoga teacher. All the CMs were like, "What? Really?? Nia, you in a zen state and not giving orders or supervising?" Linda, an invited guest, shared with us that there was a Groupon for the studio, called Dehya Yoga Studios, in Laurelton. Well, when Nia heard the name of the studio, she perked up and shared with the group that "dehya" in Jamaican patois means *right here*, and this is where she wanted and needed to be: right there, on the mat, at a yoga studio. On this evening, at this birthday potluck, Nia came alive.

Linda Chong

You know, God is a funny God. He will send someone in your life to force you to question your own beliefs and thoughts. Linda Chong *was* the one. Nia's birthday potluck changed the energy of the group. Was it bad energy? No, just a different one. Besides the obligatory white momma, Jessica, our group was full of staunch Democrat voters. Our parents and grandparents were Democrats; they wore their choice like a badge of honor. We wanted to be the change, and we were. Voting secured the future: the schools; staff; STEM and STEAM programs, manicured homes; and traffic lights at the famous "Suicide" crossing intersection where local high schoolers on any given day could be mowed down like roadkill so that drunk drivers could catch a green light. When we voted, it was for library programs, budgets, and issues which mattered not only today, but notably, five years from now.

For these reasons we all reacted with surprise when Linda entered - the most straightforward persona of all the Chocolate Mommas: tall; long hair; designer digs from head to toe; beautiful smile; thin;

divorced; no children; and a proud Trump supporter. Linda carried her support for Trump proudly and happily challenged you to reconsider getting the COVID-19 vaccine because everything was fake news and Democrats were simply pushing their agenda (as if Republicans weren't). She was an anomaly: Black; educated; Caribbean; and drinking all the Trump Kool-Aid. However, it was Linda, an avid bargain shopper who lives and breathes Groupon, who introduced the group to the new Black-owned yoga studio. Nia jumped on it and never looked back. Linda started talking about yoga and suggested the group consider a class for an outing. The CMs agreed and Nia began acting differently and relaxed after that birthday potluck.

This Color Sucks

Grey filled the sky this day - no color, no feeling, and no motivation. How do you not recognize yourself? Each day, you walk past the mirror and glimpse your reflection. If it looks decent, you keep on walking, but, today, some necessary *craziness* took hold of Nia; everything looked unfamiliar to her. Her beautiful mane was dry, filled with split ends; the gray hair multiplied like chia seeds. The skin was dry, and the pussy too. The joints were a tad achy on this day. Her eyes, smile, face, and body language all screamed something unfamiliar. What was happening, or how long has this been happening, was Nia's thought. Was she really sad, depressed, and lonely? "Wait, how long has this feeling been here?" she asked herself. "Why did someone not intervene and ask if everything was okay with me? How long have I been invisible to myself?" she queried. As she faced the mirror, it talked back to her internally saying she had given up on being happy for so long the external couldn't fake it anymore. Nia cried. She felt empty and alone, although she wasn't the only one carrying a heavy self-imposed burden.

Half of the CMs were going through some similar shit. Stuff was happening to them also. Your body will remind you when you stop caring about yourself. It's not good enough to excel in your role as a caretaker, mommy, and partner. You fuckin' matter!

Today was the moment to sit, shit, sleep, and stew in personal stuff. For Black folk living in Elmont, feeling invisible was no big thing - it was the price paid for living in a tony suburb. However, there are moments when you pray to be seen. This was one of those days. Maybe if someone had asked her if she was doing okay, she wouldn't have studied the mirror longer. Perhaps, perhaps not. Nia had spiraled into depression since she had asked for a divorce - from euphoria to sadness in mere weeks.

Winnie was dealing with health issues and wanted to be left alone. Whitley was experiencing seasonal depression and jumped off the grid. Jessica was facing the unraveling of her marriage. Christie and Zora and Linda were living their best lives and wanted no part of this CM funkdafied party. They decided to keep to themselves. The mirror will always be your friend and speak to you authentically - mainly when you lie to yourself.

Zora Love

Dark chocolate-colored skin, tall, svelte, a traffic stopper, and well-accentuated hair, she embodied the entire mood and full stop in a sentence. Men and women loved them some Zora Love. As her name declared, she was one-of-a-kind, punctuated and memorable like her momma's inspiration, Zora Neale Hurston. Zora was the last of many offspring from her momma and daddy and, as expected, floundered in the pecking order. Zora clawed for everything and managed it with love, wit, and determination, which is how she came by her last name - Love.

Shit was never easy for her, but one second, one conversation, one drink and you fell in love with Ms. Zora - if only she felt the same way about herself. She and Nia bonded the first time they met at the skating rink. Their individual personalities were big enough. They shrunk and lifted the room simultaneously. You wanted to be in their presence, however, you quickly learned their world belonged to *them* - a world which cemented the connection Zora and Nia felt. They laughed, cried, swapped childhood war stories, and motivated each other to move into uncomfortable emotional spaces.

Zora was not an original CM, but Nia refused to disregard her. Zora, who lived in another town, described herself as a baby-momma, psychiatrist, independent woman, well-traveled homeowner, a teller of truth—*always*. Nia loved those things about Zora - her mouth, sass, attitude, and drive - and she knew Zora would cut someone for her. Nia, unaccustomed to such loyalty, always kept Zora by her side. They were each other's muse, confidant, sister, judge, jury, and mirror, hidden from outer perusals. When they were together, however, their combined presence was so overwhelmingly intoxicating you gladly accepted an iota of *whatever* they offered. Sadly, they kept their magic hidden from the cosmos for the duration. They were still discovering and seeking validation from the world. Zora desired love and protection. Although not really a tall order for most women, for Chocolate Mommas, it ain't easy to come by on a daily basis. You have to commit to the inner work, pray, and then hope one day you will indeed receive what you give so freely to others: your children; parents; siblings; friends; man; partner, and job. The magical four-letter word that Zora sought to discover: *LOVE*.

Stillness is Movement

Although pondering it, Nia did not mention the word "D" - divorce - to her then-husband. He, too, was contemplating it, but didn't dare say it. The relationship had entered a new phase: separation and inequality, with separate groceries and claimed spaces in the house.

A thick, somber atmosphere permeated the air. As the tension grew, the question of who would sleep in the main bedroom arose, but to Nia, the answer was clear - the room belonged to her. Despite the pretense for the children's sake, the atmosphere in their Cape house transformed from a loving home to a lonely abode.

Feeling gutted by the misery of their children, Nia questioned the point of staying together if it continued to cause damage and create unhappiness. She put on her yoga tights and a faded *Black Girl Magic tee-shirt, grabbed* her mat, and headed to Dehya Yoga Studios to seek solace and healing. Dehya, a gem in the community, brought magic to the predominantly Caribbean neighborhood, providing a space for Black individuals to move and release.

The studio's name, Jamaican slang for "mi de ya" or "I am here," resonated with Nia's quest for perspective and flow.

Entering Dehya, Nia's energy shifted thanks to the lingering scent of Palo Santo and music by India Arie (precisely the song *Strength, Courage & Wisdom*), and the strong presence of the owner, Syntyche, Syn, as her students affectionately called her. She saw Nia's essence floating between pain, joy, love, and possibilities. Inspired by tonight's class and flow, Nia signed up for Yoga Teacher Training (200 hours) without a second thought. Tonight's mission was empowerment, happiness, and healing. Movement in body, mind, and soul became Nia's chosen path, finding stillness on a mat supported by the earth.

During Sukhasana or easy sitting pose, a loving asana is done by sitting on the buttocks, crossing the legs, and keeping the spine straight to settle the mind and become present. Nia checked in with herself, inhaling for four seconds, holding for three, and exhaling for four. Encouraged by her ancestor's whispers, she embraced her breathing, clearing space for release and answers. Releasing her body and closing her eyes, the mat enveloped her pain, inviting Nia to create a new narrative. By holding her inhalation longer, the exhalation turned into a release. Tears fell as she moved into child's pose, granting herself grace to unpack her burdens and invite a new start. Feeling the movement and hope within, Nia acknowledged it was time to break the generational trauma and take a leap of faith. The decision to ask for a divorce loomed, a choice which, prayerfully, promised to deliver movement and hope to her life.

Nia's Love for Yoga

Nia's love for yoga became a steadfast anchor in her daily routine, starting with the first rays of the morning and concluding with the dusk of nightfall. Her initial encounter with yoga occurred at age 27 in a random studio, surrounded by unfamiliar faces. Despite feeling overlooked by the instructor, the class boasted a magnetic quality that drew Nia into an unexplored realm within herself. This inexplicable connection left her yearning for more.

The turning point came in 1995, when, at 28, Nia joined a transformative and memorable yoga class in the New York City Village. The venue for the class: an unassuming setting of a bookstore with a hidden Yoga studio in the back and the Caucasian instructor who infused life, love, and soul into the practice. This experience marked a profound realization for Nia – she and yoga were inextricably intertwined, which was okay.

While it took years for yoga to become a regular practice, Nia seized every opportunity to engage in it across various cities, boroughs, states, and countries. Throughout her journey, she noted a conspicuous absence of teachers of color, even in practices like Bikram (also known as Hot Yoga). It wasn't until she discovered Yoga instructors from India at the YMCA in Bellerose, Queens, that she found a profound connection. Their teaching transcended expectations, transporting Nia's body to a euphoria where all its elements harmonized.

For Nia, Yoga became a tool for her physical well-being and a means of tapping into her mental and emotional reservoirs. As she contemplated journaling her feelings and navigating the uncertainty of self-doubt, the yoga mat emerged as a magical space. Whenever self-doubt innocuously crept in, Nia turned to the mat, finding solace and clarity in the practice. Driven to deepen her yoga practice, Nia pursued a 200-hour certification. Before this, yoga played a crucial role in saving her from postpartum depression and panic attacks.

Following her daughter's birth, her therapist recommended Bikram, pushing her to confront anxiety and train her mind to focus on the present. While Bikram provided valuable lessons in staying present, the physical toll and the demands of breastfeeding led Nia to continue exploring, seeking the best Yoga flow, studio, and instructor to complement her journey from bitter to better.

Ground Centered

A seasoned entrepreneur with a business lineage, Nia initially found her calling in middle school. Starting with baking cakes for her neighborhood peers, she gradually transitioned into a summer business selling cakes and lemonade, creating a secret haven for the local kids to gather and connect.

After a successful career in corporate America, Nia ventured into entrepreneurship, establishing her shop, Rewind Media. At age 55, having worked for herself for years, Nia prioritized her children despite the challenges. Seeking constant stimulation and change, she stumbled upon Ground Central Coffee in Lynbrook, Long Island, during a pivotal meet-up three years ago.

At the time, Nia juggled the thought of a divorce while facing uncertainties about her life. Feeling lost and depressed, she found comfort in each visit to Ground Central, which she affectionately renamed Ground Centered. With its inviting ambiance, vintage decor, and welcoming atmosphere, the coffee shop became Nia's refuge for self-reflection and planning. The space gave her hope and a sense of stillness amid life's upheavals. Frequenting Ground Central twice a week, Nia utilized it as a workstation for her Public Relations (PR) consulting projects, providing inspiration and stimulation from the establishment's natural light, pulsating music, and diverse energy.

Despite being private, Nia hesitated to share this gem, wishing to keep it all to herself. However, her friend Sasha experienced a devastating loss—her husband's sudden death and Nia suggested a check-in. Recognizing the need for sister-girl support, Nia introduced Sasha to Ground Central, turning it into a sanctuary for them both. In this coffee bar, they found a safe space to share their struggles, dreams, disappointments, hopes, and prayers.

As the epicenter of their growth and healing, Ground Central became where Nia and Sasha met weekly to meditate, eat, and release. During the pandemic, as the world seemingly stopped, the coffee bar remained a stabilizing constant, guiding Nia through pivotal moments of her life. From praying about her divorce to envisioning a new future, Ground Central became 'Ground Centered', playing a crucial role in Nia's journey, teaching her the power of mindfulness and focused thought and providing growth during each visit.

The COVID Years

In the days leading up to the Coronavirus shutdown, Nia vividly recalled working in Philadelphia, accompanied by her daughter at Fox-29 on *Good Day Philadelphia*. Her clients, the multi-talented Christian McBride and poet legendary Sonia Sanchez, were promoting an album and scheduled to perform on campus at the University of Pennsylvania later that night. Having previously worked with Sister Sonia Sanchez during her time as Jill Scott's publicist, Nia held a deep and immense admiration for her.

Approaching Sister Sanchez for a hug, Nia was surprised when she received a fist bump instead. Sanchez explained that she had just visited Paris, and a severe virus loomed on the horizon, prompting the issuance of a memo to avoid physical contact. This conversation left an indelible mark on Nia, raising the question of the situation's seriousness. Little did she know how soon the world would be upside down.

Following their time in Philly, Nia and her daughter drove to Hershey, PA, to enjoy one last vacation at the Hotel Hershey, unaware it would count as one of the final carefree trips before the onset of COVID. Fast forward to March 15, 2020 - the day the world stopped. Schools closed, and businesses shut down and halted. Hospitals faced overwhelming patient loads, and according to *The New York Times*, 1.07 million deaths were reported in the United States from the virus. Amid the chaos, Nia found herself navigating another new reality. Divorce had become finalized, and the plan of selling the home she shared with her ex-husband was thwarted by the pandemic, forcing them to cohabitate longer and face the challenges of this "new normal." Their son returned home from college for virtual classes, and their daughter attended school via Google Classroom, mirroring the adjustments made in countless households.

In the face of uncertainties about selling the house, financial stability as a publicist, and the well-being of her family, Nia turned to a familiar coping mechanism, which became a pivotal career move, tapping into the wellness industry. She found solace in walks, meditation, and teaching Yoga classes at the local park. Although COVID created a cascade of challenges for Nia, how would the house sell amid a shutdown? What opportunities were there for a publicist during a pandemic? How could she coexist with her ex-hubby in the same home while waiting to sell their home? What about the mental health of her and her kids? She also knew this was a prime time to get still and create new opportunities for herself.

Real Talk

What the future held for Nia posed a monumental question. Having battled depression for the past seven years and now recently divorced, the pandemic, oddly enough, presented a fresh start for her. Nia felt that a higher force had made the world stop, causing significant losses and collective suffering. COVID, she believed, reset the environment, pushing people to learn new skills and think outside the box, and sadly, intensifying hatred towards Black people through various incidents and the tragic murder of George Floyd. In Nia's opinion, Juneteenth would not have become a national holiday without the outrage surrounding his death, and many programs for Black entrepreneurs would have remained unfunded. The combination of COVID and George, the Minnesota man's death, was a game changer.

The world's shutdown compelled Nia to reevaluate her life and envision new possibilities. Her soul, dormant for so long, became unrecognizable in the mirror. Stress, she realized, robbed her of joy, aged her, emptied her, and threatened her very existence. Determined to avoid this bleak existence, the suddenness of the pandemic served as a wake-up call. Nia decided to take action, to fight for herself, and to be present in the moment. She chose to create a new state, a new journey. Focusing on Yoga, Nia volunteered her services to frontline workers and prioritized her happiness.

Choosing healing opened up unexpected opportunities for Nia, such as invitations to present Wellness, Mindfulness, and Yoga webinars for corporations, groups, and individuals, providing a new revenue stream. Nia further expanded her skills by becoming certified in Reiki and taking an introductory nutrition course. A new Nia emerged, which marked a significant shift in her life. As a certified yoga instructor, Nia yearned for a bigger stage. Those who truly knew her recognized her desire for growth, offered motivation and encouragement and shared their contacts, a gesture Nia considered monumental. Grateful for her sisters who prayed with her and helped her visualize a bigger world during the pandemic, Nia saw a place where she could reinvent, stretch, profit, and still find peace with a smile.

The unexpected, she learned, often came from surprising sources. Amid the pandemic, Nia remembered that breathing - the power of inhaling to take in energy and exhaling to release what no longer serves - is the only thing that separates the living from the non-living. Harnessing the power of breath became a daily practice for Nia, fueling her through the best and worst moments. As she looked forward, she encouraged everyone not to take their ability to breathe for granted, urging them to release the unpredictability from COVID and embrace each day moving forward.

Never Hold Back Your Tears and Dreams

One morning, at 53, Nia discovered a woman in the mirror she no longer recognized. Her lines and lips were hers, but the sparkle in her eyes had dimmed. The voice within urged her, "Don't hold back your tears and dreams." In response, she allowed herself to cry, releasing ugggggllly tears, a cathartic purge that breathed life into dormant dreams or paved the way for new ones. Nia always held her dreams close, a collection of aspirations nestled in her heart—some dating back to childhood, others born anew with time.

Nia knew she had to confront the good and the not-so-good within her to release it. The baggage she clung to, no longer serving her, held her hostage in her face, body, mind, and soul. Looking down, she conversed with herself, seeking difficult questions and receiving honest answers. God spoke to her in this vulnerable state, guiding the necessary pivot.

Nia and God engaged in a dialogue in the bathroom. As she faced the mirror, God urged her to embrace discomfort, challenging her to do what made her most uncomfortable—posting videos on social media and sharing personal stories. Nia, hesitant, expressed her fear, having just found comfort in posting on LinkedIn. God reminded her of her expertise in orchestrating campaigns for superstars and companies, emphasizing that this reluctance was her self-imposed Achilles heel.

Acknowledging the changing times and her evolved role beyond being a publicist, God pressed her further. Nia raised concerns about consistency and daily commitments, but God reminded her that discomfort was a superpower. She possessed a unique gift for communication, a magic that needed to be shared. It was time to let go of fear and embrace vulnerability.

Approaching 55, Nia found herself grappling with the complexities of middle age. Peeling back the layers of her skin evolved into an aggressive experience, as the mirror reflected not just physical changes—wrinkles, sagginess, discoloration, and more—but a raw revelation of self. In this moment, she saw herself like never before, acknowledging the emotions and stories from the pages she skipped over, the challenges she avoided or hid from herself. She found resonance in an Emmy award telecast, listening to winner Sheryl Lee Ralph's words - *"To anyone who has ever, ever, had a dream and thought your dream wasn't, couldn't wouldn't come true, I am here to tell you that this is what believing looks like, this is what striving looks like, and don't you ever, ever give up."*

God's message was clear...With over 50 years of groundwork, it was Nia's turn to bloom. God's plans for her were grander than her own. Gratefully accepting the guidance, Nia committed to taking baby steps on this new journey.

The Move

Nia's life had been unraveling for years. The court granted the divorce she wanted. She felt so many conflicted emotions: excited, nervous, scared, and depressed. These feelings were not new; she had been navigating them for years. The realization of her freedom, however, completely overwhelmed her. What did "free" really mean? Nia had been doing her own thing and groove her entire life. Now, with stillness, it was time to create a new chapter and initiate the following journey: let her hair down, go big, chart her path, live her best life, and break generational trauma—none of these things she processed quickly. But, the scariest thought was being alone and middle-aged. Nia's sadness fell on her like an old, heavy woolen blanket; an ending is just that: an ending.

With Nia's divorce came the natural demise of relationships from the marriage, which in turn affected friendships, not-so-great thoughts, and, honestly, a sense of impending death. "Divorce is not the end, but in the beginning, you feel like there is a sudden darkness in your life. I am not going to invite anxiety and depression back into my life. It didn't serve me in the emergency room, and now, as a divorced woman, I will not entertain it. I plan to invoke breathing, movement, and talking to my therapist to visualize, accept, and do better," she told herself. Nia vowed not to accept FEAR as her new husband, thus governing her choices. She knew it would not be easy, but the more time she had to sit with her latest title - Ms. Nia Morris, instead of Mrs. - the more she embraced the most critical change *not* celebrated or understood: a change of marital status. She realized breathing *was still* possible. Nia thought, "Who cares about judgment from others?" She had just delivered to her children the end of a marriage, a circumstance too significant to ignore. Nia's divorce signaled the end of a generational cycle of dysfunctional unions in her family. She did not stay in something because it was familiar or was protocol. Her decision amounted to a considerable feat. Although sad about the end of her marriage, this was entirely about the *emancipation* from generational trauma. Nia said, "You don't have to stay in something because your mom, auntie, and cousin did. There was an opportunity to move and remix the next move." And this is what Nia did.

It wasn't easy for her to sell her home during the pandemic, but she did. Nia and her husband agreed on a price for the sale, but cohabiting during the pandemic took stress to a whole new level, and confusion reigned for many days. It took eleven months, countless open houses, and a couple of bidding wars, but finally, their home had a buyer, making the entire process real for Nia. There was a "hurry up and wait" feeling when the realtor and lawyer gave a clear deadline for the close date. Nia cried happily, although she had no clue what to do next. She did not have a place for her and Taylor to live, and as the primary custodian of her teenager, she needed to create a plan that no longer interrupted Taylor's life. Nia knew only one viable option: to ask her mother if she could stay there for a little while - just enough time for Taylor to finish school and Nia to find a home.

The next few months would be stressful for Nia. Moving into her mother's house was uncomfortable, but necessary for growing and shedding: sharing a bed with her daughter, living in her childhood home again, and proving to herself that she could do it.

Nia was doing double duty, trying to figure out all of this. As she would later say, "The in between time in life is when all the shit resurfaces. All the things you have worked on in therapy, begin to resurface." I was doing my best to breathe, be a good parent, co-parent, and wrap my head around all this newness. However, I felt in-flux: sad; depressed; and lost. My friendships, once strong, were now MIA. Thank goodness for being open to new friendships in a new space. I have always heard that friends change as you age. It happens for a day, a season, a reason, or a lifetime.

The pressing issue remained finding a place to call my own; definitely not a space where I am on borrowed time and feel like stale fish, or the unwanted guest. People asked me what motivates me? I simply replied, *life*. Defying the odds. Seeing my children smile. My belief in God and his promises which say you have to experience loss to experience life. I know that I am in transition, and this too shall pass. But, let me tell you, I am not coming back to this space or place.

It's Happening

Nia was happy when the mortgage broker's call confirmed the Clear to Close date. It had felt like forever, but the delay only lasted a few weeks. Her living situation at her mom's continued to weigh heavily on her shoulders. It was best described as a fragile and tenuous coexistence. Now, the weight has lifted. Nia sat on the bed she shared with her daughter and cried. The tears streamed down her face - tears of joy, pain, release, validation, and expectations. It was a good cry, an excellent cry for Nia, and one that was important for cleansing and resetting. She couldn't wait to tell the Chocolate Mommas, but Taylor, her baby girl, deserved to hear the news first.

Taylor had just graduated from 8th grade, and Nia chose to stay at her mom's house to keep Taylor's routine. Lawdy- what a sacrifice, but Nia was grateful. Talk about a challenge in patience and grace. Nia shared the great news with Taylor, and they both screamed and danced happily. Nia's "to-do" list for the move looked daunting, like registering Taylor for a new school in a new state, eliminating and donating clothes and placing the significant stuff in storage, and mentally and physically letting go to create space for the new journey. She could *finally* share the move with CMs, family, and friends. Her ex-hubby knew it was imminent. With the sale of the family home, her ex-husband's spirits soared. He had already moved and started the next phase of his life. Surprisingly, they were both moving to the same state - Connecticut. For the first time, in forever, they both acknowledged this was reset time. Although the marriage ended, they both dedicated themselves to their children and demonstrated the best version of themselves for the next chapter. The physical move was happening in two weeks.

As Nia orchestrated the relocation to Connecticut, Chocolate Mommas, old and new (some members had moved and others had joined), planned a surprise soiree in her honor. Nia's heartstrings tugged when she arrived at the soiree; it surprised her. When she saw the beautiful array of food, gifts, and wine on display, she allowed herself the release of all her pent-up emotions. It started as a smile, a thank-you speech, and finally, a good, gut-wrenching cry, not just about the move or the soiree. It was all of it: the marriage, the divorce, selling the home, buying a new home, moving to a *new* state, and feeling wholly depleted and overwhelmed. It was a lot to process for Nia. As she looked at the CMs they had on their best and brightest summer wear, Nia thought, "When you find a circle of women who see you, hold them tight."

Nia was going to be okay. She managed to do all these things one baby step at a time. It was necessary to take these tiny steps and create milestones to grow. She knew The Chocolate Mommas always had her back, along with friends and family. Nia felt that the move would bring uncertainty for her and Taylor, but shit, the past several years had been predictable, and all it did was to give her a slow death sentence. She wiped the tears, looked at Winnie, Jessica, Zora, Whitley, Christie, and the crew, and said, "Thank you. I have been in a haze for so long, and each of you poured life, encouragement, tough talk, and love. Chocolate Mommas, you rock! It is time for me to make this move and live. I appreciate you for seeing this complex, beautiful, and nervous Black woman in her 50s moving to a new space and place and helping me grow from bitter to better. I love you all."

A New Beginning

When Nia first moved to Connecticut, she was overwhelmed. She described how she felt like she had an out-of-body experience daily. The condo made an unfamiliar sound at night. The grocery store did not have her favorites and familiar Caribbean items, and the nights felt strangely different. The new queen-sized bed seemed big—and empty—after sharing it with her ex-husband for sixteen years.

As for friends, what friends? Only she and Taylor traversed this journey; they would have to figure out how to manage it. Thankfully, Taylor was still seeing her therapist via Teletherapy (Nia stopped since moving to Connecticut. She knew her toolbox was fully armed if she followed the steps. 1) Communication, 2) Clarity, 3) Consistency, 4) Adaptability, 5) Transparency. Nia had made it a point to say what she wanted to say and mean it.

Initially, the Chocolate Mommas checked in on Nia and visited her several times. Real talk though; the distance was a pain in the butt. It took three hours on some occasions to get to a gathering. It was no secret Nia wanted the divorce, so all the CMs figured she was okay and living her best life - not true. Nia was navigating her new routine and getting her career back on track. Nia told Winnie she would curate the life she always wanted to live with purpose: *Think big. Live boldly. Breathe.* Dismantle the generational trauma to yield the best version of herself and her family. Nia said, "I will give myself time to relearn what I like and dislike as a divorced middle-aged woman. Taylor and I will sink our teeth into everything this new town offers." Meet new friends, grow together, cry together, and accept the ultimate goal of blissfulness. Her new mantra was "Not perfection or balance, but simply bliss. Finding something to feel good about daily in our new space." These words encompassed the mission - a tall order but not an impossible one.

After spending 25-plus years as an award-winning Media Strategist, Nia debated whether or not she planned to spend another second doing that. Although she loved her career as a publicist, Wellness and Yoga were her joy. However, the prospect of pivoting to the wellness arena unsettled her; she truly understood her potential and possessed the acumen to thrive in the *corporate* wellness field, but with so many variables. Nia was a survivor - a work-in-progress like many women, navigating trauma, postpartum depression, panic attacks, and anxiety. Therapy and movement saved her life, and now, having taught Yoga and Mindfulness for two years and working as a corporate trainer, Nia wanted to help others. Whenever she taught a yoga class or spoke about mindfulness, she also healed the body and mind by harnessing calm. Nia thought, "I can go hard with this clean, new slate. Why not get my 500-hour RYT, write a best-selling book, and become a Top 5 Wellness and Motivation speaker?"

Nia knew it would not be easy to cross off those goals from her list, but what was stopping her? She had been cultivating and demonstrating her talents; she was an exceptional speaker. She made her clients feel special, allowing them to see themselves as larger than life. Today represented the start of something new, and Nia only had to please *herself* this time.

Ode to Friendship

The driving force for us all is unconditional love. Not being judged, feeling supported, seen, held, loved, challenged, and having a safe space to be yourself simply – warts and all. With all of Nia's accomplishments, she was exceptionally proud of her tribe, circle, and friends - people she had rocked with since middle school. How lucky! Nia curated the most delicious people in her circle from each intersection of her life: from the seventh grade, high school, college, her first job, the music industry, consultancy, entrepreneurial endeavors, as PTA president and School Board member, Mocha Moms; and now as a Yoga instructor. All the friendships had value, but the one as a mother and wife helped her navigate truly rough terrain, and the bond she shared with her Chocolate Mommas was a special gift. They all had war - and victory - stories. The women's ages now range from the mid-40s to 60s. Each had something to offer the other and knew that laughter would always get them through the challenging times. As a collective group, they had mourned the sudden death of a spouse and bonded with divorces, medical procedures, layoffs, moves, and fresh starts. Despite all these things, they managed to circumnavigate the most challenging situations to the most fun, eventually reveling in celebratory ones. Everything from spa retreats, birthdays celebrated around the continent, Zoom mental health check-ins, wine tasting, salsa dancing, sad goodbyes to a loved one's parent, paint and sip, concerts, children's recitals, and graduation, countless dinners, potlucks with our waistline to prove, and a shitload of phone calls to bitch, moan, and just be. Nia created the Chocolate Mommas and crafted a sisterhood—a real sisterhood, not that fake stuff where you sit around and gossip.

Not so Good Today

Zora felt poorly today, which had been happening for a while. Her blood sugar was up, and she was struggling to manage the diabetes. After years of minimally following the doctor's to-do list for the diagnosis, the worst knocked loudly at Zora's door. The friends just wanted to stay in denial; it was too much for anyone to handle now. Nia and Zora were the ultimate Thelma and Louise, the perfect Ying to the other's Yang. Still, recently, with Nia managing a divorce and selling her home, she was unable to process another damn thing.

Zora did not want to burden Nia with more stuff, so they kept pretending their worlds were not imploding. Zora ghosted folks while going through something; Nia remained the more communicative friend. However, Nia needed her friend to talk things through, listen, and laugh; Zora had retreated. Zora was fighting to live, which took precedence over Nia's current issues. Nia always had abandonment issues; she knew her dad; well, she met him three times, but he wasn't around, and her mom had told Nia that he died when she was thirteen or fourteen (another story for another time) and that stayed with Nia when dealing with people. However, Nia always felt she could count on Zora, no matter what since they had always been there for one another. Zora's silence did not sit well with the other Chocolate Mammas either; Winnie, Whitley, and Christie kept trying to give her time. Nia didn't understand why Zora was M.I.A., but she gave her the needed space. For both of them, generational trauma - part of their respective legacies - had reared its ugly head—pain, strife, drama, and trauma. Nia would say that Black women come out of the womb with trauma. They carry the stress from their parents, especially their mothers, as soon as they are born. Zora and Nia lamented their relationship with their mothers, yet they always looked for their approval. Although today was not a good day for Zora, she was determined to do a little more.

Maybe call Nia and check in? After all this time of avoiding Nia, she missed her. What would she say to her dear friend for not reaching out, not taking her calls, and avoiding her? What was there to say? Zora did not anticipate getting sick; who *plans* to get sick? She was knocked off her ass for two years and then disappeared, which produced consequences from the outside world - living a compromised life with an ailment equals loss of time, relationships, friendships, and self. Zora had to fight to return to self, and today felt suitable to reach out to Nia with a quick but necessary conversation. Zora picked up the phone and dialed. The ringing felt like forever, and Zora prayed that Nia would not pick up the phone. Zora took a deep breath and let go of her internal conversation as the phone continued to ring, "No more; I need my friend, and she needs me too. I'll start with a simple 'hello' and let it flow from there." The salutation was all it took for Zora and Nia to start talking. They stayed on the phone for a few minutes, with Zora slowly building up her courage; those minutes felt like an hour to them both. They cried, laughed, prayed, shared, and released some of the pain and heaviness they had carried in their silence. The beauty of a Chocolate Momma friendship is its realness. It is not cute or for show; this is a sisterhood/friendship, and it is messy because *life* is messy.

Add Chocolate Mommas to the mix because they will have your back unconditionally - and the recipe for navigating life because you know shit can go sideways in a nanosecond, especially when you least expect it. The longer you live, the more you realize that life is complicated and brings all kinds of things: good, bad, indifferent, sad, happy, sickness, recovery, loss, and joy. All of these offer a barometer for what is happening internally rather than externally. Zora and Nia had to endure different life stuff, but the common denominator is *stress*.

Their stressors were through the roof, almost costing them their joy and lives. Be intentional with the people you choose to be around, ask for what you need, and understand the seasonality of life.

Everything in life has a season, including friendships, but the best of sisterhood will endure the summer, spring, fall, and winter. Zora and Nia remain besties - even when their friendship takes an unplanned hiatus.

A Chocolate Momma's Journey to Self-Discovery Soulful Offerings for daily use.

MEDITATION FOR MORNING AND NIGHT:

"Today, and only today, is what matters. I will inhale everything that I know is good about life and my choices. Grace is all I ask for in exchange." Breathe in/out and scan your body; allow it to settle. With each breath, inhale calm, light, forgiveness, and peace. Slowly exhale forgiveness, angst, depression, and all that no longer works. If it compromises my spirit, it no longer serves me. Breath in/out, in/out, in/out.

AFFIRMATION:

Today, and only today matters. One breath at a time.

AFFIRMATION FOR UNCERTAINTY:

I know this will pass. My mindset is expansive, and I will feel what I need to feel and let go. I can pivot, reframe my mind, and relax my body for the better. Better is waiting for me. Repeat: Better is waiting for me.

AFFIRMATION FOR PEACE:

All is well. All is well. All is well.

AFFIRMATION FOR CLARITY:

Stillness is where all the magic lies. I will communicate with my mind, body, and spirit and ask, "What's going on?"

AFFIRMATION FOR DAILY MANIFESTATION:

Thank you.

AFFIRMATION FOR GROWTH:

I am grateful for the disappointments; they allowed me to receive the yummy.

MEDITATION FOR MENTAL PEACE:

Close your eyes or relax your face. Bring your awareness into the present tense, and permit yourself to feel. Relax the shoulders, torso, legs, and breathe. Bring your attention to your mental peace; that is all that matters. Keep repeating to yourself or out loud that my mental peace is all that matters. I am grateful for my mental peace. I am thankful for my mental peace. Keep repeating: inhale light, peace, and joy through the nose. Count to three and hold your breath for four counts. Gently open your lips and exhale it all. Let go of what you no longer need. Repeat this as needed.

AFFIRMATION FOR MOTIVATION:

I am doing my best with today's information.
All I can do is my best.

AFFIRMATION FOR DAILY ATTRACTION:

I am very blessed. Abundance is my birthright.

AFFIRMATION FOR DAILY BALANCE:

My self-care is my soul care.

AFFIRMATION TO REDUCE STRESS:

I have permission to be just as I am.

AFFIRMATION FOR SUPPORT CHECK-IN:

My _____ is/are my rock. Thank you for rocking with me with no judgments.

Icons designed by Freepik

MEDITATION FOR CLARITY

Burn a stick of Palo Santo in your safe space and sanctuary.

Repeat 3x: "I am doing the best that I can with the information I have."
Sit/lie comfortably on the mat, hands at your side.

Whatever your uncertainties, ask for clarity and let it go with grace.
Breathe in through the nose (four counts).

Hold your breath (four counts).

Exhale through the nose (six counts).

Continue this sequence until you feel your face and muscles softening.
Whatever your uncertainties, ask for clarity, and then ask the
question.

Tap into the power of your inhalation to bring energy into your body
and the exhalations to release the stale air and bring renewal and
space as you let go.

Soulful Yoga
Practice for Soul-Care
(Can be done with a chair)

Sit comfortably on your mat and close your eyes or whatever is comfortable. In Sukhasana pose (Criss-cross applesauce), sit with your spine upright and relax your shoulders, face, arms, and legs.

Take a breath (pranayama). Inhale through the nose, and count to three, expand the abdomen, hold it, and exhale slowly through the mouth to count my voice as you draw the navel and stomach in. **(DO THIS 3X)**

Set an intention now.
It can be as simple as to stay present in your practice.

WARM-UP
Swing your legs around, moving your legs and back around in a circular flow, getting low to the ground if possible to release all the stress and tightness in your body. Continue to move at your pace. **REPEAT 4X ON EACH SIDE.**

As we continue to warm up the body, let's flow into the cat/cow. Take the time to breathe into this pose and incorporate your feet as you tap into your inner cat. **REPEAT 4X.**

Stand up and come to the front of your mat. Feet are hip length apart. Relax your body in Mountain Pose (Tadasana), standing tall, and bring your hands to your heart. Breathe into this position. **HOLD FOR THREE (3) DEEP BREATHS.**

Keep your feet hip width apart, take your hands from the heart center, and bring them above your head to meet the sun with a sun salutation. Relax your shoulder, breathe, and stay there for a count of three complete breaths. Now, place your hands on the floor, to ground yourself, allowing the breath to flow, being intentional with feeling your toes, the mat, or whatever feels comfortable. Move your hands to your knees as you breathe, and a big exhale back to your heart space with hands together. **REPEAT 3X, AND REMEMBER TO BREATHE.**

Now that you feel warm from your sun salutation, stay in the pose longer by hinging your feet, moving your legs to the mat (gently), and doing a child pose. **Breathe here.**

Move your legs from the child pose and get into your first downward-facing dog. Stay here and breathe.

Stay in a downward-facing dog, move your upper body forward, and get into a plank pose (or as close as possible). **BREATHE HERE FOR THREE (3) FULL BREATHS.**

From a downward-facing dog, bring your knees down on the mat, move your right foot back, and come into a low lunge. Align your body, which should feel good—a nice stretch and reward. **BREATHE HERE FOR 2 FULL BREATHS. LET'S DO THE SAME THING ON THE NEXT SIDE: GET BACK INTO THE DOWNWARD-FACING DOG, COME DOWN ON THE KNEES, AND BRING THE LEFT FOOT BACK. BREATHE FOR 3 FULL BREATHS HERE.**

Get up slowly. Bring your feet together and go back to mountain pose. Take your arms and gently move left to right to release the last bit of stress. Relax everything here and breathe. Keep your legs hip width apart, come up on your toes, and give love to the ankle. **REPEAT THIS 2X.**

Come down on your mat, and bring your body to a bridge pose. **Stay here for TWO (2) FULL BREATHS. REPEAT THIS 2X**

Come down on your mat fully, bring your legs to happy baby, or do whatever you must to feel like your practice is complete before Shavasana. Get what you need now, like socks, a sweater, a blanket, or a block.

You are ready to reward your mind, body, and soul. Completely relax, let go of the mind chatter, breathe. Let it go. You came here today to honor yourself; remember that. Congratulate yourself for being courageous. It is brave to put yourself first. You did that as you intensified your breathing and channeled pranayama: deep inhalation, pause, and exhalation. Remember to use this time to inhale all the goodness of your life. And, deeply exhale whatever doesn't work. You've earned it.

STAY HERE FOR FIVE (5) MINUTES DEEP IN YOUR THOUGHTS. IF THE MIND CHATTER COMES, START COUNTING DOWN FROM ELEVEN (11).

Get ready to move around your toes, legs, arms, neck, face, and smile. Sit up in Sukhasana pose (Criss-cross applesauce) and breathe. If you have an intention, remember what it is and call upon it throughout the day and as needed.

May the light in you shine bright as you take what you need from this class to sparkle.

Namaste.

Notes for a Chocolate Momma on a Journey to Self-Discovery:

Acknowledgments

My journey has been made special by countless remarkable individuals' wisdom, encouragement, and support. I stand on the shoulders of these giants, whose contributions to my life and work cannot be overstated! While I endeavor to express my gratitude to each of them, I am mindful that some names might inadvertently be omitted. For this oversight, I request your understanding and grace.

From the onset, certain people have left an indelible mark on my heart and my path. Ms. Boruso, my high school English teacher, deserves special mention for planting the seed of storytelling within me as far back as 1985. Uncle Oswald, whose inquiries about my book remained constant until his untimely departure, and Rodney Lofton, my brother in love, and sweet Angela Pittman, all of whom have left us too soon, continue to inspire me from beyond.

My editor, Astrid Roy Pinto, has supported me and encouraged me to remain faithful to my authentic self—a gift for which I am immensely grateful. Andrew, my ex-husband, consistently motivated me to persevere and bring this project to fruition, a testament to the power of enduring support despite our marriage ending.

I am also blessed to have been embraced by an extraordinary community of "Chocolate Mommas"—Gilda, Sharron, Sabrina, LaTanya, Agnes, Mangy-Nkoli, Janet S, Janet T, Wendy, Pam, Khadija, Ann B, Audrey B, Denise, Sandra, Nicole, Redhead, Dyana, Lynette, Tawana, Michelle, Tracey, Sheila, Sonia, Shannon, Daphne, Sabrina H, Lorna, Kay-Ann, Tiffany, Christine, Tonia, Vikki, Syreeta, Aisha, Tonya P, Jen Armstrong, Patty J, Kiesha, Sherise, Fatima, Gina, Angie, Guashauna Nixon, Latrece Robinson, Nyla Williams, Llana Bowen, and Suzanne Cooke. Each of you, in your unique way, has enriched my life with warmth, wisdom, and unwavering encouragement. Syntyche', the extraordinary woman who reintroduced me to myself through yoga, holds a special place on this journey. Similarly, the beautiful souls at Discovery Place School—staff and students alike—have offered me a platform to teach yoga and love freely, fostering an environment of growth and healing.

Finally, to all the yogis who have trusted me to guide them, sharing the sacred space of the mat, your faith in me has been a source of soulful joy and fulfillment. Thank you from the bottom of my heart.

About the Author

D edicated to empowering individuals to live their best lives, Karen Taylor Bass is a reckoning force. With a contagious joy and a deep sense of purpose, she is an award-winning media strategist, activist, author, and inspirational speaker.

As a certified Yoga Instructor (RYT-500) and Meditation leader with a concentration in Trauma-Informed Yoga, Karen brings authenticity and compassion to her clients. Drawing on her own ability to overcome adversity, she motivates and inspires others to tap into their inner strength and resilience.

Karen is also a Corporate Wellness Trainer, working with organizations to develop and implement programs which improve employee health and productivity. Her certificate in Reiki from North-well Hospital in Long Island further enhances her expertise in the wellness field.

Karen is the creator of the annual International Soulful Yoga Day, a celebration of mindfulness, self-care, and community. Her work has been featured in numerous media outlets, including *The Wall Street Journal*, *Washington Post*, Sirius XM, *Essence*, *AARP Magazine*, Fox News, and The Dr. Oz Show.

Request Karen Taylor Bass as a Speaker/Keynote/Presenter

TaylorMade Books are available at quantity discounts with bulk purchases for educational, business and sales promotional use. For information, please contact: info@taylormademediapr.com.

Find more at:

Website: KarenTaylorBass.com

Instagram: @KarenTaylorBass

Instagram: @SoulfulYogawithKaren

YouTube: KarenTaylorBassYoga

www.ingramcontent.com/pod-product-compliance
Lightning Source LLC
Chambersburg PA
CBHW070328120726
47909CB00008B/2644